LEROY COLLINS LEON COUNTY PUBLIC LIBRARY

3 1260 01003 2350

AR-No Test

W9-ANY-506

A BOY'S BEST FRIEND

For Augusta, a girl's best friend

This book could not have been done without the help of our
friends and neighbors: Nicky Camerato and his parents Mary
and Nicholas, Natalie Michaels, Travis Ursprung,
Jason Woodruff, Michael Wyant, Kristine Monahan,
Justin Whitbeck, Frances Smith and Mitzi, Dee Myers and
Moffat, Diane Dunn and Bounce, Linda Vidinha and Caleb
and Cleo, and our friend Nancy Ursprung who always says
yes. We also appreciate the encouragement of Sasha Alyson
and LeDogg, who pointed us down the dog path in the first
place.

—J.A. & C.H.

Copyright © 1992 by Joan Alden. All rights reserved.
Photographs copyright © 1992 by Catherine Hopkins.
Typeset in the United States of America; printed in Hong Kong.

Published in hardcover by Alyson Publications, Inc.,
40 Plympton St., Boston, Mass. 02118.
Distributed in England by GMP Publishers,
P.O. Box 247, London, N17 9QR, England.

First edition, first printing: September 1992

ISBN 1-55583-203-2

A BOY'S BEST FRIEND

By Joan Alden

Illustrated by Catherine Hopkins

ALYSON WONDERLAND

Will is nearly seven years old. He lives in the country outside Montreal with his mother and her friend, Jeanne Martineau, who is French Canadian. Every year since Will was four he has asked for a dog for his birthday. And each year he has been given something else and told it was for his own good.

It's bad enough to be teased at school because he cannot play ball. It is even worse to be denied a pet because he has asthma. A dog is a boy's best friend, and Will could use a best friend.

E Ald
001003 2350   LJB
Alden, Joan.

A boy's best friend /

   10-17-2000   SDW

LeRoy Collins Leon County
PUBLIC LIBRARY
200 West Park Avenue
Tallahassee, Florida 32301-7720

A few days before Will's seventh birthday, he announces to his mother and Jeanne that if he cannot have a dog for his birthday he wants nothing at all.

On the morning of Will's seventh birthday there is no gift at his place at the breakfast table.

At school Will's classmates sing happy birthday. Usually the birthday boy runs around the room while the others sing to him, but Will doesn't have enough breath to run. He has to stay in his seat. Will doesn't like being different, but there's nothing he can do about it. He *is* different.

At home that evening, Will blows out the candles of his birthday cake, making the same wish he has made for four years. As Will is tucked into bed by his mother, he feels especially lonely this night. His seventh birthday has come and gone and he has received no present. Now Will is sorry he demanded a dog. Then Jeanne appears with a big white box tied with a blue ribbon.

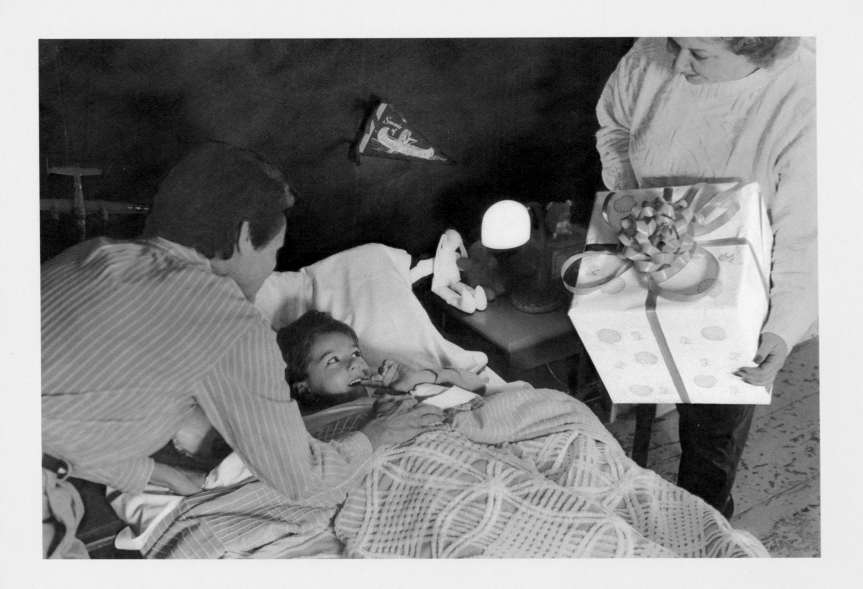

Will sits up in bed and shakes the box. It makes no sound. Will puts his nose up to it and sniffs. It doesn't smell like a dog.

But to Will's great surprise, when he opens the box he sees the button eyes of a woolly dog looking back at him. Engraved on the dog's tag is the name LeDogg. On the back of the tag is Will's address and telephone number.

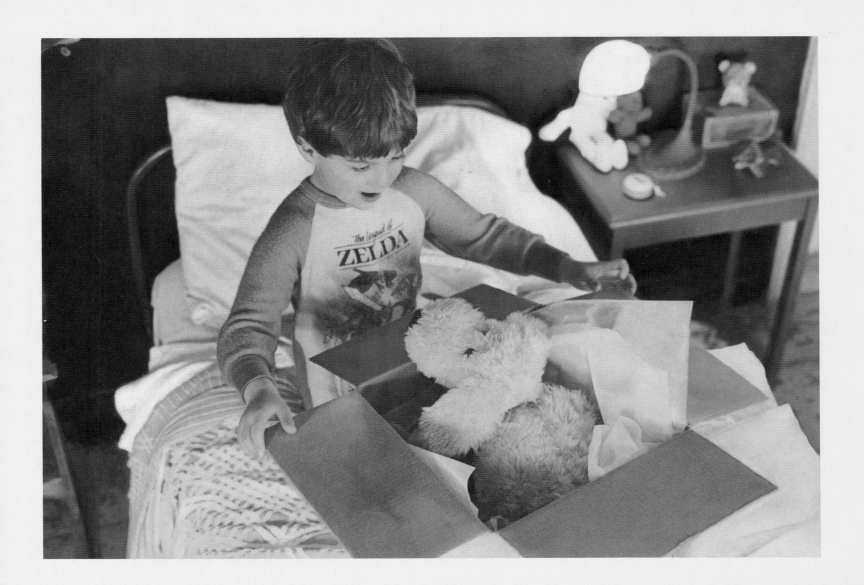

Will and LeDogg sleep together. In Will's dream, LeDogg and Will run up a grassy hill. At the top of the hill there is an airplane waiting for them. Will and LeDogg climb in and fly over Montreal, passing Will's house. Jeanne and Will's mom are in the backyard, waving to them.

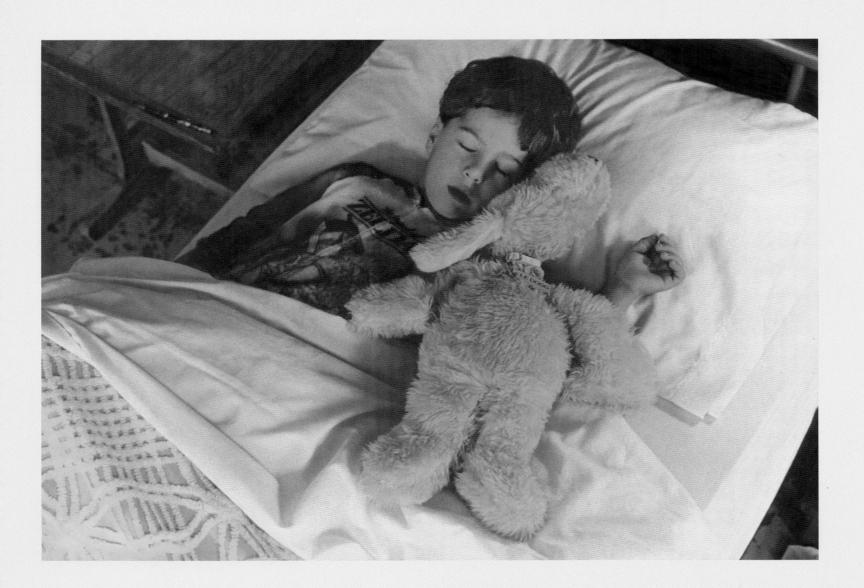

The next day is Saturday, and Will takes LeDogg to the park. The park is a popular place. LeDogg meets a border collie, a golden retriever, and two dachshunds.

When LeDogg lies down on the picnic blanket, he puts his head on Will's leg, and Will feels love in a way he has never felt before. Will has no words for it.

On Sunday LeDogg goes to church with Will. Before going inside with his mom and Jeanne, Will ties LeDogg to the iron fence. Inside, Will sings the hymns to LeDogg.

Monday morning, as Will is dressing for school, he realizes LeDogg will have to stay at home. Dogs are not allowed on buses unless they are seeing-eye dogs. LeDogg is different than other dogs, but not in that way. LeDogg can't bark, or run away, and he doesn't smell like a dog. Will could hide LeDogg in a shopping bag and no one would know he had LeDogg on the bus with him. Will asks LeDogg if he would like to go to school with him and he knows the answer is yes even though LeDogg cannot wag his tail.

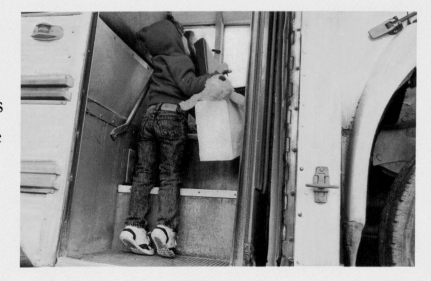

At school LeDogg stays in Will's locker until lunchtime when Will takes him to the playground. Some older boys tease Will about his strange dog. "Let's see him fetch!" a boy squawks.

When LeDogg doesn't chase after the stick, another boy boy squeals, "He's a willy-nilly dog!"

In unison, several boys chant, "Willy-nilly! Willy-nilly! Willy-nilly!"

Will returns LeDogg to his locker. It was not a good idea to take LeDogg to the playground where he suffered the embarrassment of being poked fun at. After this, Will will leave LeDogg at home.

After school, Will waits for the bus to take him home. One of the bullies catches sight of LeDogg's tail sticking out of the shopping bag and reaches for it. Will pulls away, but the bag tears. Before Will can catch hold of LeDogg, the bully has him.

LeDogg is pitched into the air. LeDogg is stretched and pulled and tossed from bully to bully while Will cries out for his dog and the bus leaves without him.

LeDogg sails over the tree
tops. He is caught by a bully and
hurled again, this time plunging
straight down through the
branches of a tree and getting
caught on a limb. The bully
taunts Will to climb to LeDogg's
rescue.

Will walks over to the tree, takes a deep breath, and
calls up to LeDogg, "Come!" Then he coughs, takes another
deep breath, and calls again, "Come!"

This time LeDogg leaps from the branch and lands in
Will's arms. Will hugs LeDogg to him, then, smiling broadly,
Will walks home.

At dinner Jeanne asks Will, "How do you think LeDogg was able to jump from the tree?"

"I think it was something supernatural, something that doesn't mind that LeDogg is different."

"Everyone is different," Will's mom says. "When you don't mind your difference it stops being a problem and becomes your distinction."

Will has heard this before, but today he understood. Today he wasn't hurt by the name calling. He was only concerned about LeDogg. Today, even if he could have, Will wouldn't have changed himself into one of the bully boys.

LeDogg lies on Will's chest in bed while Jeanne reads a bedtime story. When the story is finished and the light turned off, Jeanne and Will's mom whisper, "Sweet dreams," and tiptoe out of the room.

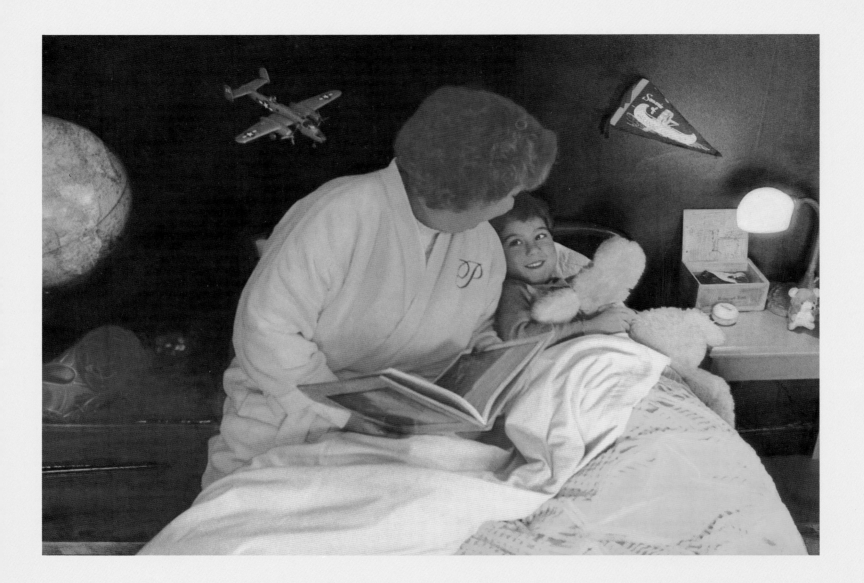

Alone in the dark, Will feels a soft, wet tongue lick his cheek.

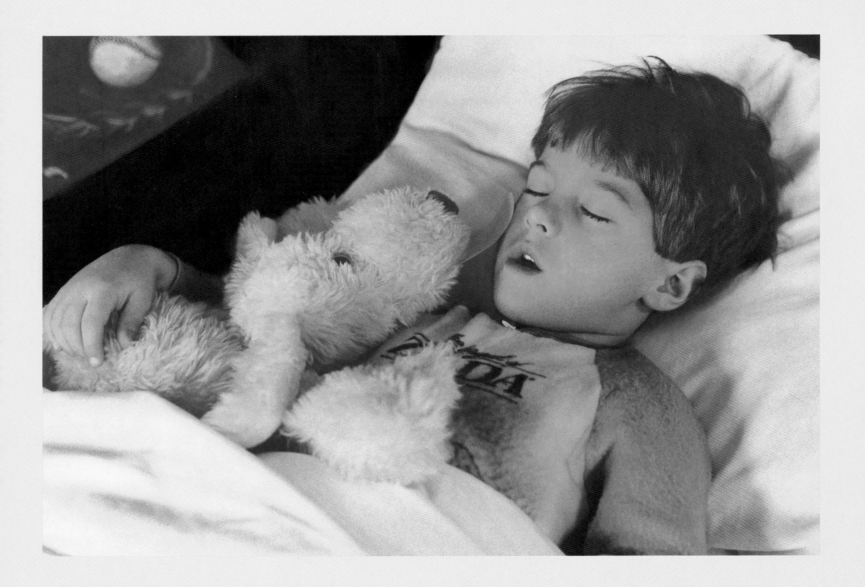

For information about our other children's books,
please request a free Alyson Wonderland catalog from:
Alyson Publications
40 Plympton St.
Boston, Mass. 02118